INK[illegible],
The Barn Cat

MW00892823

Elizabeth Bernaski

illustrated by Marina Hierl

Copyright © 2009 Elizabeth Bernaski
All rights reserved.

ISBN: 1-4392-0960-X
ISBN-13: 9781439209608

Visit www.booksurge.com to order additional copies.

 FOREWORD 

Liz Bernaski, a volunteer at Equi-librium and an elementary school Reading Instructional Assistant, has created a story about the very special horses and children at Equi-librium. Equi-librium is a NARHA Accredited equine assisted activities program that uses the horse to help children and adults experience positive changes physically, mentally, and emotionally. The horse's movement and the human-horse bond are very powerful and supportive to those with disabilities. Liz's story, narrated by Inky, our barn cat, tells about some of our special horses, how they help, and some of the activities that take place. It is hoped that this story will bring to young readers an understanding and an appreciation of what we do, and of those with special needs.

To learn more about Equi-librium visit our website at www.equi-librium.org or contact us at:

Equi-librium, Inc.
P.O. Box 305
Sciota, PA 18354
570-992-7722

THIS BOOK IS DEDICATED TO

"Jake"

Jake (on the left) and his best friend, Sam

and **"Lacey"**

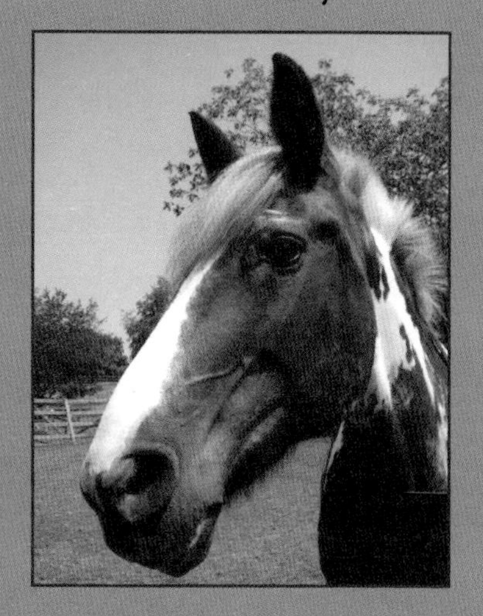

Both were loved by all and are truly missed.

Thank you to A.P. for sharing her pictures.

Inky

My name is Inky, the Barn Cat. I live in a big barn with my animal friends. The day I came to live here, everyone called me "Inky" because my soft fur looks like black ink! I have a very important job at the barn, and that is to run fast and chase the little mice away! I really like my job!

I am so glad you came to visit me today. My life at the barn is very exciting, and we can spend the day with my best friends. Would you like to meet them? Let's go!

Inky and Her Friends

I live in a big barn with nice horses. We are all good friends and we have fun together. I want you to meet my best friend, Sam.

Sam

Sam is a very big horse! But he is a gentle horse. He loves when the children come to ride on his strong back for their lesson. Sam's job is to help a little boy or girl learn how to ride. It is a very important job. Sam is patient and kind to everyone. That is why all the children love him!

Lil' Bear is a friend of mine, too. He is not as big as any of the other horses. His coat is brown and black with a little bit of white on his back.

Lil' Bear

Lil' Bear is a *Miniature horse*, which means he is only 34 inches tall! How tall are you?

Lil' Bear is very strong because his job is to pull a cart around the barn with one or two people in it.

He is very good at his job. He likes to get carrots when he is done with his work. Lil' Bear is my friend too.

This is my friend, Diamond. He is not as tall as Sam, but he is not as small as Lil' Bear. A lot of children ride him because he is just the right size for them. Diamond is strong too. He has a white mane and tail, and nice eyes.

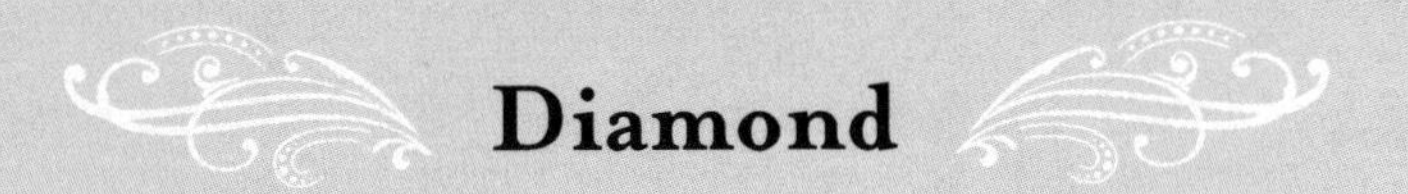

Diamond

He likes to play and run when he is outside in the pasture. When it is time to come in and work, Diamond is ready to do his job. He is very calm with the children when they are riding him and he always gets a big hug at the end of each lesson.

Let's go say "Hi!" to my friend, Lacey. She is a very pretty horse with brown and white patches on her coat. She loves to have children ride on her back too, just like Sam. Lacey is always careful when the children are riding because she knows they are her friends. She works hard at her job too. I like to sit in the top of the barn and watch Lacey when she is working.

Lacey

Sometimes Lacey has a little cough, just like people get. She has asthma, and she gets medicine to make her feel better.

Does that happen to you? When she gets her medicine, she feels so much better. I am glad she is my friend.

Meet my friend, Michell. She is one of the *instructors* for the students who come up each day to ride their favorite horse. Her job is to take care of the horses, keep them healthy, and to keep everybody safe. It is a very important job.

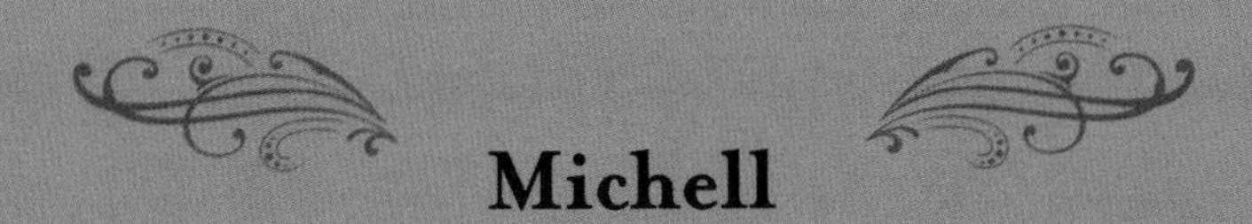

Michell

When you come to the barn for the first time, Michell is very careful to make sure that you wear your *safety equipment* before you even get on your horse.

Just like at school, you have to follow the rules at the barn when you are around the horses and while you are riding.

Here comes my friend, Kenny. His mom brings him to the barn every week to ride. It is time for his riding lesson. First he has to put a *safety helmet* on his head and a *safety belt* around his waist.

Kenny

Kenny is going to ride Ben today. He has to remember to be calm, quiet and gentle when he is ready to ride.

Okay, we are ready to go!

Today he has a *sidehelper* to make sure he is safe by walking along the side of the horse. He has another important person, the *horse leader*, to guide, or lead, his horse around the arena while he is learning how to ride. The *horse leader* and Michell bring Ben around for Kenny to gently get on his back .

Exercises

"It's time to do your exercises," said Jody, the *sidehelper*. So Kenny sits up straight and begins his exercises. He puts his arms straight up in the air. He learns how to keep his balance and sit quietly on Ben's strong back.

Kenny cannot walk like other children because his legs are not very strong. But when he rides a horse, he can do many different things.

"Would you like to play a game?" asks Jody, the *sidehelper*. "Do you like to play basketball?" she asks. Kenny is good at this game - he can throw the ball in the hoop every time!

 **Playing basketball** 

He can also catch the ball when Jody tosses it to him. "Good catch!" says Jody. Ben stands very still and calm while Kenny is playing basketball.

When the game is over, Kenny tells Ben to *'Walk on'*, and Ben starts walking forward. When Kenny wants Ben to stop, he says, *'Whoa'*. Ben knows what Kenny is telling him and he listens very well.

Big hugs!

Soon Kenny's riding lesson is over for today - what a lot of fun he had!! He gives Ben a big hug around his neck because he did such a good job!

I am so glad you came to visit me today! My good friends at the barn were very happy to meet you.

(stretch) It is time for me to take a nap. We have had a busy day! I hope you can come back to visit me again. See you soon!

Words I know

Miniature horse: A horse that is 38 inches tall or smaller.**

Instructors: The people who make sure that you wear the proper equipment and teach the riding lesson.

Safety equipment: The items you wear to keep you safe while you are riding.

Safety helmet: The riding hat you wear during your lesson and when you are around your horse.

Safety belt: The belt that goes around your waist during your lesson and while you are around your horse.

Sidehelper: The person who walks along the side of the horse during your lesson to keep you safe.

Horse leader: The person who guides your horse around the arena.

'Walk on' : What you tell your horse when you want to go forward.

'Whoa' : What you tell your horse when you want to stop.

**I would like to thank M.R. for her assistance on this page.

About the author

Elizabeth Bernaski works in an elementary school assisting students with their reading and writing skills. One of the things that gives Liz great joy is to see a child read and enjoy a good book!

In her spare time, Liz has been a volunteer for four years at the Equi-librium barn where she combines her love of horses and working with students. She is the mother of three grown children, and her husband of over 26 years is very supportive of all her volunteer activities. Liz would like to thank everyone who has been involved in the creation of this story about the children who participate in the Equine Assisted Activity and Therapy program and the horses that they love.

About the illustrator

Marina Hierl has been volunteering with Equi-librium for six years. Three days a week she comes to the barn and helps students with their riding lessons or does any work that needs to be done around the barn to help take care of the horses. When all the chores are finished she likes to spend time with and ride her own horse, Gigi. She has been riding and taking lessons at Equi-librium for all six years. Marina is currently in high school.

Made in the USA